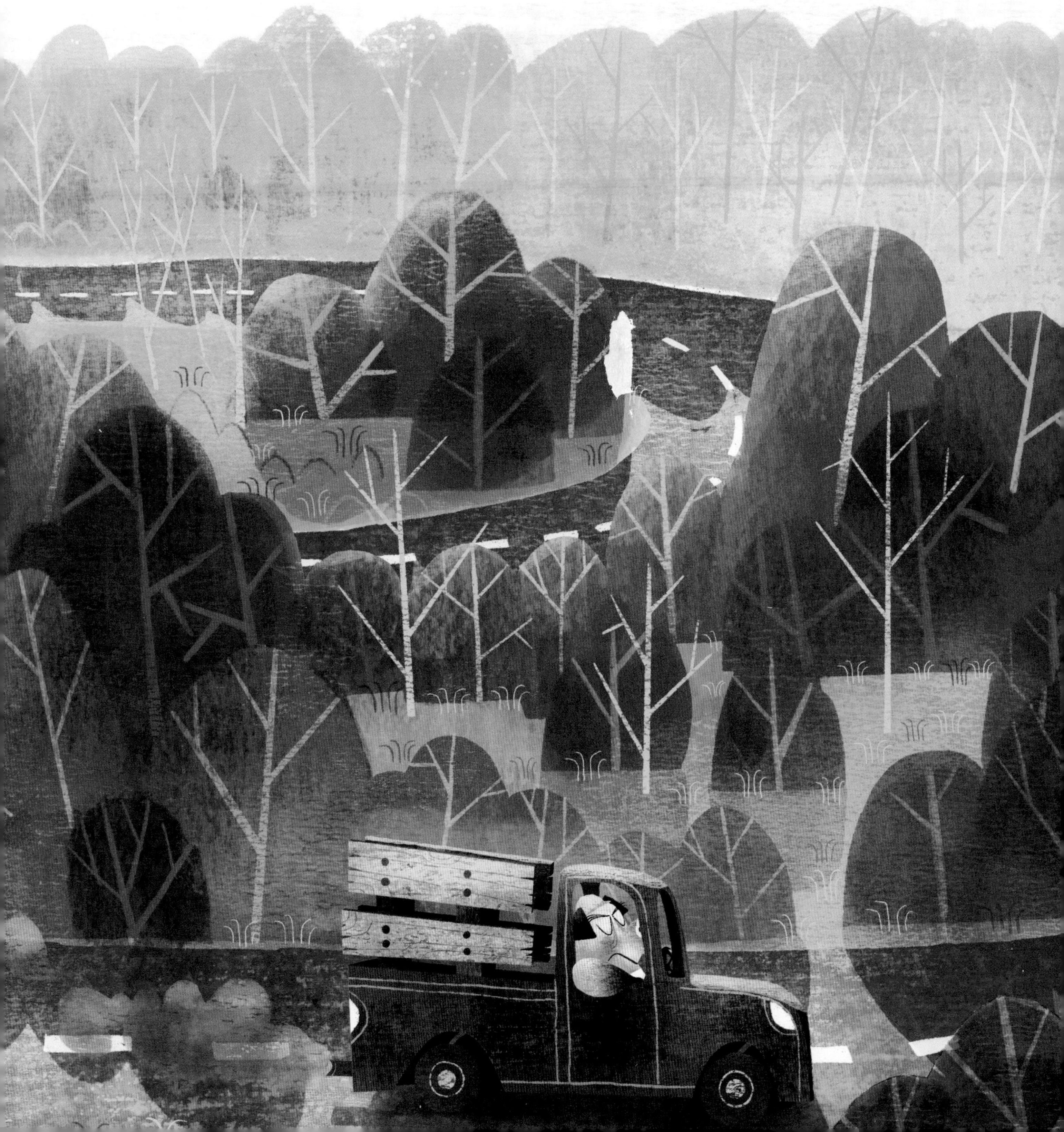

For Vanessa and Leo

Copyright © 2020 by Glenn Hernández
All rights reserved. Published in the United States by Random House Children's Books, a division of Penguin Random House LLC, New York.
Random House and the colophon are registered trademarks of Penguin Random House LLC.
Visit us on the Web! rhcbooks.com
Educators and librarians, for a variety of teaching tools, visit us at RHTeachersLibrarians.com
Library of Congress Cataloging-in-Publication Data is available upon request.
ISBN 978-1-5247-7206-2 (trade) — ISBN 978-1-5247-7207-9 (lib. bdg.) — ISBN 978-1-5247-7208-6 (ebook)
MANUFACTURED IN CHINA
10 9 8 7 6 5 4 3 2 1
First Edition
Random House Children's Books supports the First Amendment and celebrates the right to read.

Mr. Pig's Big Wall

by Glenn Hernández

Random House New York

Little Tortoise was a happy, chatty animal who loved to play.
She lived next to Mr. Pig, who was neither happy nor chatty.

He only loved his precious garden.

Little Tortoise loved Mr. Pig's garden, too.

She wanted to play and help and chat and garden.

All the time.

But Mr. Pig didn't want to play and chat and garden with her.

And he especially didn't want her help.

One day, he stopped gardening
and started a new project.

"What are you building?" asked Little Tortoise.
"A new flower bed? A new patio?"

"A firepit?"

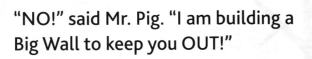

"NO!" said Mr. Pig. "I am building a
Big Wall to keep you OUT!"

And the wall grew and grew,
until it did keep Little Tortoise out.

And as the wall grew and grew,
Mr. Pig's garden fell into shadow.

When he was done building,
he climbed back down to his garden.

But he found there wasn't much garden left.

Little Tortoise was sad that her neighbor had shut himself away.

But then she had an idea!

She gathered all her supplies . . .

. . . and prepared to bring some sunshine to him.

She picked a flower for Mr. Pig, and up, up she went!

But when she pulled the flower from the wall, a huge crack began to climb up alongside her.

Mr. Pig saw the crack.
"HELP!" he cried.

And the wall
crashed down
below them.

Together they rose, and Mr. Pig could see
a world with no walls and no fences. . . .

Only beautiful flowers, trees, sunshine, and . . .

. . . chatty animals.
And that was just fine with Mr. Pig.